The First Time I Bunked My Class

Saurav Banerjee

<u>**Acknowledgements**</u>

This book is dedicated to my childhood friends of that time, who made this all happen.

And also, to all those students who often do bunk their classes for the sake of enjoyment and creating beautiful lifetime memories.

About the Book

In this book ***The First Time I Bunked My Class*** I'm going to tell you an interesting story of my childhood when I bunked my class for the first time.

The story I'm going to tell you is no one knows except of my friends of that time. Read the story ahead to find out how this all happened.

Regards: Saurav Banerjee

<u>About the author</u>

The author's name is Saurav Banerjee, and he is living in Aligarh, Uttar Pradesh (INDIA).

He has completed his high school from the SMB Inter College, Aligarh (Commerce stream)

And his intermediate from HB Inter College, Aligarh (Arts stream)

Currently he is pursuing his graduation (BA) from SV Degree College, Aligarh.

Apart from studies, he is following his passion of writing and is writing quotes and poems actively on **YourQuote.in**

Also, he has published his first book of his own written poetry collection ***Words Of Heart: English Poems*** on 5th of July 2019.

<u>Prologue</u>

Before starting this story, let me share you something related to this so that you can understand it much better.

A few days ago in my present college in which I'm pursuing my graduation, me and my friend were sitting in the library and were reading newspaper, after finishing the newspaper we decided to go to the park as our periods were off for the next two hours.

There (in park) we were talking about our subjects and their timetables. Here I'm presenting a very short part of that conversation between us.

"So Saurav, how your classes are going?" Ankit (name changed) asked

"Fine, and what about your classes?" I said

"Fine," Ankit said

"And what about your psychology classes?" Ankit asked

"Fine but I feel very awkward in that class everyday" I said

"Awkward? Why?" Ankit asked

"I often think psychology is a gender specific subject" I said

"What the.... I mean why you think?" Ankit asked after laughing for two minutes constantly.

"Because I'm the only boy in that class and the rest are girls, damn" I replied and was feeling awkward at the same time.

"Wow, that's a great thing I think" Ankit said still trying to control his laughter

"What is the 'great' in this you mean?" I asked

"You said, in that period you are the only boy and the rest are girls. Isn't it great?" Ankit said

"How?" I asked

"See, there are a lot of girls in that class and you are single, so I meant to say you might get a girlfriend soon. Congratulations in advance." Ankit said

I don't know why but sometimes I just don't get Ankit, seriously.

"How do you think I could get a girlfriend just by sitting in a class with too many girls? LOL" I said, asked actually

"Who knows one day you might start talking to girls then she'll become your friend then best friend and very gradually you'll become her boyfriend and she'll become your girlfriend" Ankit said

 "Very funny, you know I can't do all these things, I hesitate as hell" I replied

"Sometimes I wish if I could bunk this class but I couldn't because it is a practical subject" I said

"Anyway, bunking the class was your good idea but thanks, you dropped it. Now you are growing up" Ankit said

"By the way, how many times you have bunked your class?" Ankit asked

"Many times," I said

"Could you remember when you bunked your class for the first time?" Ankit asked

"Yes, very clearly," I said

"Oh, that's great, now tell me that story" Ankit said

"What... are you crazy, it's a long story bro" I replied

"Not crazy, but serious, because class bunking stories are always interesting. Now please don't keep me waiting and tell me the whole story." Ankit said excitedly

The story begins…

As far I remember, ten years ago from today in the year 2009, I was in Delhi Public School of Rajgir (a small town of Bihar near Nalanda district).

At that time, I was in my second standard and also I was not so good in my studies and was famous for not completing my home works and for sleeping during the classes.

 All I knew was to play and make fun of our every teacher during their classes sitting on the middle bench of class.

I was that type of student who never pays attention to the class and always busy in my own world.

One day our maths teacher gave us homework and told next day she'll check our homework copy so all the students complete their home works. But thankfully that next day was Sunday and it was something definitely awesome for the students like me. I thought "wow… tomorrow is Sunday; then how could she check our home works?"

Well alright, I'll try to complete my homework tomorrow on Sunday.

But as I told you before, "I was not so good in my studies" hence I forgot to complete that shit on Sunday.

Next day (on Sunday) ...

Well, that was the Sunday and I was the laziest person in my house too, so there was no chance to wake-up early in the morning.

Anyway, I woke up at near about 09:30 AM and had no idea of that homework given by our maths teacher. I had also some other subjects' homework to complete but didn't complete any of them due to my forgetfulness.

I enjoyed the Sunday to the fullest and didn't even I opened my school bag that day as I don't know if I've a school bag too to open and to complete those mind shucking home works.

In the evening I played some outdoor games with my friends and after that we went for an evening walk to visit some nearby parks and to do some fun as like racing, playing police and thief & etc.

Till now everything was going fine and awesome. That's how we enjoyed our Sunday peacefully and happily.

Ugh... wait, I'm forgetting one thing to tell you and that is really an interesting topic.

Four days before this day, I was fallen sick in the evening due to my idea of having fun as it was raining in the morning so I decided to take a bath in rain because it was the hottest summer and was totally frustrating. Our skin was burning like hell and we all were waited for the rain to come so that the temperature could fall by little.

Anyway, my parents were a little tensed about my sickness and were busy get a good doctor for my treatment but somehow I was not sad but happy for my own sickness as it was helping me to not going to school so that I could save myself from getting those useless and frustrating and boring as well home works.

And without any extra excuses I was doing my favourite thing and that was obviously, sleeping, as I was the laziest person in the house. And so, it was really a helpful incident in my favour happened to me.

The another day in the morning my parents took me to a doctor for my check-up, there was rush on road due to heavy traffic and it caused a long time taking jam but I was definitely enjoying that awesome moment in a tempo sitting on my mother's lap comfortably and my father was also there sitting beside my mother as I guessed if we reach late to the doctor, we might not be able to meet the doctor and if it happens this way I'd have not to face the fear of the injection or nor the doctor. Anyway, after half an hour we reached to the doctor's cabin and it was my bad luck that the doctor was there in his cabin as like he was just waiting for us only.

He greeted us and said to come-in and we entered his cabin and sat on the chairs, I sat on the middle chair, my mother was on left and father sat on my right side.

After few minutes he gave me some medicines and told to my parents to give those medicines on time or else it will take few more days for me to get well and recover my health as it was before.

Further he told us to come on the next day so that he could observe my health conditions if it is improving or not. The moment I heard this, I was like "what the hell, why I've to come here again tomorrow?"

Anyway, the next day it was raining again and it was a good sign for me, I thought I saved myself today from going to the doctor.

But guess what, a shit happened and the rain stopped soon than I expected it to stop. And now I'd to go to that doctor again for the check-up with my parents, there he checked me again and realized that my health is improving and will come back to normal very soon and it really happened, my health became normal by the evening but still I didn't go to school next day as the doctor suggested me to take rest for one day.

But I was not in mood to waste that day sleeping on the bed so I started to think what to do instead. After thinking for few minutes finally I thought to go to a friend's house to meet him.

Let me remind you one thing I was thinking this all while we were on the road back to home after the doctor's check-up.

Well after facing a short time traffic jam we reached to our home at around 12:30pm. After half an hour, we finished our lunch and went to take a little rest.

At around 04:30pm we woke-up and after half an hour my mother served us evening tea (milk for me) and some snacks.

After finishing my boring milk, I got ready to go to my friend's house as I planned. His house was near about 500 meters so I reached to his house in half an hour, there he was in lower and t-shirt in front of his television monitor busy with his video game playing some games which I don't remember. To playing videogames was the one of his favourite things.

The game which he was playing was a keyboard game actually. To play that game you have to connect a videogame keyboard to your television monitor and that keyboard includes a small gaming device comes with many (around 100) games stored in it. I also had a videogame keyboard in my home but I never used or you can say, I never played much with that as like my friend used to play with his videogame. He was playing some fighting games about which I had zero idea. But still he asked me to play with him; firstly, I refused to play with him because I was not good in videogames also. But after few minutes he convinced me to play one round with him but in that one round I also got addicted with his videogame. In first two-three round he won the game and from the next level I started to play with more attention and concentration, in few attempts my performance has started to improve now my score was increasing. After playing few rounds with him we decided to stop the game and then we started to talk about our studies. He had also some home works to complete, during our conversation auntie (his mother) entered the room and we took a pause in our conversation.

There his mother started to talk with me about my studies and about my parent's and grandparent's health. After talking for few minutes, she left the room and we started our conversation again.

"How your studies are going?" Pradeep (name changed) asked

"Fine but not interesting" I said

"Why? What happened?" Pradeep asked

"Nothing yaar, my home works are not completed and I was also fallen sick due to rain a days ago." I replied

"That's not good, how are you feeling now?" Pradeep asked

"Now I'm completely fine" I replied

"And what about your home works?" Pradeep asked

"Incomplete" I replied

"Would you complete your homework or not, why you are so lazy?" Pradeep asked

"Bhai, I don't like to do those crappy home works, they are too boring, and you also know that." I said

"Yes, I know that but still, if you don't complete those home works your teacher might punish you for that too. Don't you understand that?" Pradeep asked

"I'll make some excuses to save me from their punishments." I replied sarcastically

 "Okay, but what if they detect your excuse?" Pradeep asked

"Nothing like that will happen, I guess." I replied

"But what'll you do if in case it happens?" Pradeep asked

"Then what to do, simple, that teacher will give me some punishments." I replied

"Don't you fear of punishments?" Pradeep asked

"Not that much, but it seems like you do." I said

"No, I don't. But I don't like to get punishments." Pradeep said

"By the way, how many times teachers punished you?" I asked

"I don't remember the exact number... umm say, two three times." Pradeep replied

"Okay, tell me about any of the punishments you got to date." I asked

"Well, a few days ago a teacher of my class gave me a task to complete during the class. It was little difficult for me to do, as I didn't get the teacher properly. So I made a little mistake and the sad part is that the teacher's mood was off that day." Pradeep said

"Oh shit, then what happened next?" I asked

"Happened, which I didn't expect to. Firstly, that teacher slapped me and then said me to stand on the bench in hands up position." Pradeep replied (looking sad)

"And also, on that same day in another period, I got one more punishment due to my incomplete homework." Pradeep added

"What punishment you got?" I asked

"The teacher of that period sent me out of the class." He replied

"And when you went back into the class?" I asked

"A few minutes before that period end." Pradeep replied

"Ah! It's really bad. That day really went bad for you." I said

"No worries, happens sometimes, bhai." Pradeep said

"Yeah, I know."

I spent a well and quality 2-3 hours at his house. Then I decided to return back from there. On the way back to my home, I met another friend, Gagan (name changed), and had some conversations with him also.

"Hey, Saurav, where are you coming from?" Gagan asked

"Hey, I went to Pradeep's house to meet him." I replied

"Oh, that's great. But is he alright?" Gagan asked

"Yes, he is alright. I just went for a casual meeting and nothing else." I replied

"Okay, will you go to school on Monday?" Gagan asked

"Yes, definitely I'll go to the school on Monday. Why, will you not?" I asked

"I'll also go. I just wanted to confirm if you'll go or not." Gagan replied

"By the way, where are you coming from this time?" I asked

"Nothing, actually I was feeling bored at home so just came here for a walk." Gagan replied

After this, we walked along on the road, cracked some jokes, talked on some other topics like school, class teachers, subjects, classmates, friends, etc. and then we returned back to our homes.

When I came back to home, it was 7pm on the clock and it was time for some snacks hence my mother served us the same. Also, I was little late. So they asked me the reason for being late and I convinced them that on the way back to home, I met one more friend named Gagan, and was having some conversation with him. Then they said nothing.

After few minutes, my parents and grandparents asked me about my friend Pradeep, and his family, as my family were very close and familiar with his family.

After finishing my snacks, I went to my study room to do some of my school works but I forgot to do the important one.

After doing some of my school works, I (we) had our dinner and then we went to sleep.

2 days later...

And now it comes the Monday morning, damn!

In my room there was a crazy clock showing 05:30 AM and that was the time to wake-up from the dream and to come back in this real world where at your school your teachers are eagerly waiting for you to check your homework copies and the innocent students are having fear of getting punishment if their home works are not completed or if teachers find any mistakes in their copies they will surely scold them for the mistakes done by the students.

Anyway, I woke up with a tension about the homework which I have not completed.

After struggling for few minutes to calm down myself, I got ready to go to the school and within ten minutes I reached to my school.

There I met my crime in partner friend of that time named 'Himanshu' we were almost same in the nature and we had done many shits together in that school from hiding teacher's stick to stealing chalks from the staff room.

I also met with some other friends there and discussed about how could we save us from that maths teacher because she was one of the strictest teachers of our section 2nd A. Actually, there were four strict teachers in that school but she was something dangerous type teacher and this was the reason we don't wanted to face her at any cost so we planned to bunk her period of maths.

 After few minutes we made some changes in our planning and took the last bench to sit on and kept thinking about our planning.

One bad thing was our maths teacher was our class teacher too. So every day in the 1st period she used to come to take our attendance but her actual period was the 4th one.

After struggling at the assembly we all went to our classes and after few minutes she came as usually to take our attendance and we backbenchers were like "oh shit, she will definitely punish us today for not completing her homework"

After taking our attendance she went out of the class and the teacher of that period entered.

He started to continue the chapter which he didn't completed on the last day.

After teaching us continuously for thirty-five minutes, our first period finished.

Now it was the time of our second period and that period was of Drawings but the teacher of that subject was late that day so we got some extra time to discuss about our plan but damn, we couldn't, because our drawing teacher came to interrupt our planning on the midway.

For me the drawing was also a boring subject because I didn't know anything to draw but still I had to pretend like I'm not feeling bored with this subject.

He gave us a theme to draw on but I had not any idea how to draw that. That theme was something on the nature (as far I remember).

After few attempts finally I draw something on that theme but it was not good enough to impress our drawing teacher and he crossed that saying "it is not so good, you have to do some more practice and hard work to improve your drawing skills" he further added to give it one more try.

But this time I didn't do it for myself, I took help of my friend instead and my friend helped me a lot with his beautiful drawing skills.

Then I went to our drawing teacher and submitted it accepting that my friend helped me this time. Teacher appreciated it that I said him the truth. And he said it is okay but you have to learn it and also should keep practicing it at home. I said "sure sir, I will practice it at home."

This period of drawing was also finished. After this period finished, I and my friends went outside of our class to refresh ourselves as we were feeling bored in the classroom.

Now it was the time for the next (third) period which was of Science.

Well, this subject was not that much boring for me as the other subjects is (except English). But, I never scored well in this subject also. It's my unique kind of trait, ha-ha, LOL.

I'm unable to remember the chapter but it was an interesting chapter for sure. I never felt bored in this period and always enjoyed while attaining it.

It was the only period when almost the entire student of our class paid all their attention.

During the class, suddenly, the thought of maths period and its teacher came into my mind. Along with this, a sign of worry was also visible on my face. Then I looked at my friend and shared it with him. He told me, *"bro, don't worry. We all will face it together, so just chill and calm down."*

The teacher in the classroom noticed our unusual discussion and asked us what happened. But, we were not innocent students at all. So we gave some excuses to the teacher, and he also didn't force us to tell the truth.

After teaching us for more 10-15 minutes, he went out of the class as the period was over.

But we (I and my bunk partners) were in trouble now. For us, an adventure was just about to start.

It was the time for finally executing our plan, so along with that Science teacher, we also left our classroom.

We were going to downstairs and saw our maths teacher approaching towards our classroom with a stick in her hand. I guess, ma'am didn't notice us going downstairs.

Anyway, we went to the washroom to wash our sweaty faces and to calm down ourselves. In the washroom, we discussed about our bunking plan before proceeding further.

After discussing, we came out of the washroom as it was not a safe place for bunking purpose, and then one of my bunk partners said to go upstairs in order to find a safe place to bunk the class. But unfortunately, we found not a single place so that we can bunk.

But while searching, we found a quite lone place (actually it was a storeroom type classroom) so we decided to sit there and think what to do next.

There a friend came up with an idea to go to the terrace (not on the top one); we all nodded to his idea and did the same.

But there was a sad fact we were not aware of. That sad fact was, the school authorities often comes there to inspect if any student bunking their class there on that terrace.

Anyway, we went to the terrace and found a cool place to sit. After spending few minutes there we were thinking that our bunking plan is successful.

Then other students also came there for the same purpose, we got some extra company by then.

Now, five more minutes have passed and a 'shit got real' type moment was about to happen. We started to hear feet sounds approaching towards us. We all got tensed and nervous at the same time.

In that mean time, few of us managed to hide themselves in a room on that terrace very less people were aware of.

Suddenly, one of my friends got a weird idea to jump off the terrace to the second floor's balcony type roof which was connected or interlinked to a classroom, which means you've to go through a classroom to reach there.

Well, there was not that much of height between the terrace and that roof on which we thought to jump. But still, it was not safe at all.

There were high chances for any mishap to happen, because we were not even in our teens that time. And even after knowing all these things, we nodded to this idea and after thinking for a while, we jumped from there as there was not any other option left for us to choose.

After jumping from there, we checked ourselves if we are physically alright or not. Thankfully, we were all fine and in full piece. Then we decided to go inside that classroom of which roof we jumped. But then we noticed from the window's glass that in that class there were students and a teacher busy taking their class.

After seeing this, we went to the washroom of that class to hide ourselves as the 4th period was about to finish in just a few minutes. Yes, you guessed that right. In that school, there was a separate washroom in every classroom.

After spending 4-5 minutes in the washroom, our school bell rang and it was the indication that the period is now over and we succeeded in our class bunking plan too.

After hearing the bell, we said, *"whoa guys, our plan worked. Congratulations!"* together.

Then we waited for the teacher to go out of the classroom so that we can return back to our own classroom.

In our classroom, our classmates asked us *"where you guys were vanished? Ma'am was asking about you all."*

"Damn! Did you say anything to her?" I asked

"Nope, we just said that we don't know about any of you." A student replied

"Thanks, you said nothing to her about us." One of my bunk partners said

"Saurav, today we bunked our class and saved ourselves from the ma'am's punishment. But we've to make sure that tomorrow we'll submit our maths homework copies to the ma'am." Himanshu said

"Sure bro, we will." I replied

In my present college (after telling the whole story to Ankit)...

"So, Ankit, this is how and when I bunked my class for the first time. How was the story?" I asked

"Hmm bro, it was really very interesting." Ankit repied

"Have you told your parents about it?" Ankit asked

"Bhai, are you gone crazy, or are you thinking me mad?" I asked

"If they get to know about it, they'll kill me." I added while laughing at his dumb question

"Bro, please don't share this story with my parents." I said

"Just chill, bro. I'm not going to tell them anything, so don't worry at all. Relax." Ankit said

"By the way, how you all felt after bunking you're your class for the first time?" Ankit asked

"Ha-ha, well, it was the first time we bunked our class and we succeeded also, so we obviously felt like we've won a battle. And also, by doing this we learnt a very important thing of our lives." I replied

"Oh, what's that important thing?" Ankit asked

"We learned the value of the teamwork and friendship." I replied

"Could you please explain me how?" Ankit asked

"Sure. See, if in this plan my friends wouldn't have supported me, was it possible for me or to others of our partners to succeed in this plan?" I asked

"It was absolutely not possible." Ankit replied

"And also, if we were not united as team for this plan, would we able to execute it successfully?" I asked

"Nope." Ankit replied

"This is how we learnt these things." I replied

"Yes bro, I agree with you." Ankit replied

And we have passed one and a half hour sitting at the college's park and discussing about class bunking story.

"When your next class is?" Ankit asked

"After thirty minutes." I replied

"And yours?" I asked

"Same. After thirty minutes." Ankit replied

'What to do till then?" We both asked in unison

"Should we sleep here?" Ankit asked in a sarcastic way

"I don't know about you but if I sleep here, I won't be able to attain my next class. And it'll also be called a bunk class. LOL." I replied

"Ha-ha, same with me." Ankit said

"Then, what to do?" Ankit asked

"What about taking a walk in the ground?" I asked

"No bhai, don't know why today I'm feeling tired." Ankit replied

We spent our more fifteen minutes discussing 'what to do next.' Then we decided to let our ass be stick to the bench as our asses were.

Then our classes were about to start, we decided to leave that place and go to our classrooms.

When we started to move, we saw two students were coming towards the park with the same motive to bunk their classes (we guessed it by their body language).

"Now they are coming to create their own 'class bunking' memory." Ankit said laughingly with a tone of sarcasm.

THE END...

www.ingramcontent.com/pod-product-compliance
Lightning Source LLC
Chambersburg PA
CBHW021405160726
47994CB00007B/3090